# THE BOONSVILLE
# BOMBERS

Weekly Reader Book Club Presents

# THE
# BOONSVILLE
# BOMBERS

## ALISON CRAGIN HERZIG

*Illustrated by Dan Andreasen*

**VIKING**

This book is a presentation of Newfield Publications, Inc. Newfield Publications offers
book clubs for children from preschool through high school. For further information
write to: **Newfield Publications, Inc.**, 4343 Equity Drive, Columbus, Ohio 43228.

Published by arrangement with Viking Penguin, a division of Penguin Books USA Inc.
Newfield Publications is a trademark of Newfield Publications, Inc. Weekly Reader is a
federally registered trademark of Weekly Reader Corporation.

VIKING
Published by the Penguin Group
Viking Penguin, a division of Penguin Books USA Inc.,
375 Hudson Street, New York, New York 10014, U.S.A.
Penguin Books Ltd, 27 Wrights Lane, London W8 5TZ, England
Penguin Books Australia Ltd, Ringwood, Victoria, Australia
Penguin Books Canada Ltd, 2801 John Street, Markham, Ontario, Canada L3R 1B4
Penguin Books (N.Z.) Ltd, 182–190 Wairau Road, Auckland 10, New Zealand

Penguin Books Ltd, Registered Offices: Harmondsworth, Middlesex, England

First published in 1991 by Viking Penguin, a division of Penguin Books USA Inc.
1   3   5   7   9   10   8   6   4   2
Copyright © Alison Cragin Herzig, 1991
All rights reserved

LIBRARY OF CONGRESS CATALOG CARD NUMBER: 90-50568
ISBN: 0-670-83595-1
Printed in the United States of America
Set in Caledonia

In baseball
the loyal fans in the stands
are often referred to
as the "tenth player."
So this book is for
Elizabeth Winthrop, my tenth player,
and for all those
who ever played the game
on the green green grass
of Ebbets Field.

# CHAPTER ONE

Emma Lee Benson loved to play baseball.

"You're just like your Aunt Esther," said Mrs. Benson.

"I guess that's why she gave me her hat," Emma said.

Emma loved the faded red baseball cap. Her aunt Esther, who had moved to New York City, sent it to her in the mail.

*Dear Emma,* Aunt Esther had written on the card. *The buildings here are huge, but*

*my apartment is as small as a mouse hole.*
*This is the cap I wore when I was ten like*
*you. I'm passing it on because there is no*
*room for anything in my closet.*

The cap fit perfectly. Emma wore it night
and day, except at meals.

"Hats off," Mr. Benson said. "Time to say
grace."

"Aw, Dad, do I have to?" Michael said.
Michael was Emma's older brother. His
baseball cap was black with a green bill. "I've
got a really bad haircut."

"Off," said Mrs. Benson.

Emma didn't think Michael's haircut was
so bad. She wished her hair was blonde and
straight, too, not dark and curly. She wanted
to be just like him. But most of all, she
wanted to play on his baseball team.

It wasn't exactly a team. There was only
Michael and four of his friends from the sixth
grade. But they all had team T-shirts. Michael had made them with his stencil set.

He lettered BOONSVILLE BOMBERS on the front with black Magic Marker. On the back, he had drawn airplanes with bombs dropping out of them.

"Let me wash that shirt," Mrs. Benson said about a hundred times a week. "It's beginning to smell."

"No way," Michael said. "You'll ruin it."

"Michael, do you want to drive your mother crazy?" Mr. Benson said.

But Michael just folded his arms across his chest. "The Magic Marker will run," he said.

Secretly Emma hoped her mother would wash it. Then, maybe, if it really was ruined, Michael would give it to her and make himself a new one. Even if the letters dripped a little, it would still be a Bombers T-shirt. And then, when she had a T-shirt, she planned to ask Michael if she could play.

Emma had a three-part plan for becoming a Boonsville Bomber.

The T-shirt was the first part of Emma's plan.

Saving up to buy a baseball glove was the second part. The cheapest glove she could find at the mall cost $15.95. Emma had saved $4.50. She kept the money in an old sock hidden in her underpants drawer.

Practice was the last part. Every day after school, Emma practiced her throwing and fielding. She threw an old tennis ball against the side of the house. When school let out for the summer she practiced in the morning, too. She even practiced before breakfast.

"Emma," Mrs. Benson said, "why don't you call some of your friends? See if they want to come over and play?"

"They don't like baseball," Emma said.

"Emma," Mr. Benson said, "the sound of that tennis ball is driving us crazy."

Emma felt bad about driving them crazy.

So she waited until her father left for work and her mother went to the market or the mall or next door for a cup of coffee. Then she pulled the brim of her baseball cap down over her eyes, picked up the tennis ball, and went out to the backyard again.

Michael played with the Bombers every afternoon. But sometimes he would practice with her after supper, before it got too dark to see. He even let her use his real baseball. Emma loved the hard smooth feel of it and the way the seam curved and looped in an unbroken line.

Michael taught her to throw with her shoulder and her wrist, not just her arm. He taught her to bend her knees and keep her bottom down when she went after grounders.

"You're pretty small," he said one evening in the middle of July. "But you've got good hands."

Emma beamed. "Really, Mikey?"

"And you're quick and fast," Michael said. "For a kid."

Emma peered at him. His Bombers T-shirt was covered with spots. A new blob of what looked like spaghetti sauce stained the front. Her mother would definitely have to wash it. Probably soon.

"If I'm that good, do you think I could play with you sometime?" Emma asked.

"You just did," Michael said.

"I don't mean here," Emma said. "I mean play with your team. If I had a Bombers T-shirt and everything," she added quickly.

"No way," Michael said.

"But you only have one fielder. And you don't have a second baseman or a third baseman or anything. I could be one of those."

"We don't need more bases," Michael said. "We have it all figured out. First base and home is a double. First base and home twice is a home run."

"I could play shortstop, maybe," Emma said. "That would keep a lot of balls from going through. And I wouldn't have to bat. I don't care about that."

"But you don't have a glove. And we're one glove short already."

"I don't care about that, either. Please, Mikey. Just once. Okay?"

"No way," Michael said. "You have to have a T-shirt. No one can play out of uniform. It's regulations."

"But what if I find one somewhere," Emma said. "Can I play then?"

Michael grinned. "Sure. If you find one."

"Gee, Mikey, thanks." Emma wanted to hug him, but she didn't. Michael hated hugging. "You won't be sorry. Promise!"

"I know," Michael said. "I only made five T-shirts and I'm not making any more."

# CHAPTER TWO

When Emma came down to breakfast two days later, the washing machine was going. She listened to the slosh while she ate her cereal.

Michael was still asleep.

Emma watched her mother load the pile of wet clothes into the dryer. Then she dug her tennis ball out of the umbrella stand and went to play one-man catch in the backyard. She threw the ball as high as she could and circled under it until it came down. Some players just let the ball drop into their glove. Michael called that "nonchalanting it." He said you could make a lot of errors that way. Every time, Emma was careful to catch the ball with both hands.

After a while, she heard shouting from the kitchen.

"How could you, Mom! That was my shirt!" Michael yelled.

"It wasn't a shirt," Mrs. Benson said. "It was a walking garbage pail."

Emma tiptoed up the porch steps and stood outside the screen door.

"But I told you," Michael yelled. "Now look at it. It's totally wrecked!"

"It doesn't look wrecked to me," Mrs. Benson said. "It looks nice and white again. And the letters didn't run. They're as clear as can be."

"But it's shrunk!" Michael howled. "Can't you see?"

"It is a bit smaller," Mrs. Benson said.

"Smaller!" Michael shouted. "It's the size of a pot holder!"

"Maybe it will stretch out when you wear it," Mrs. Benson said.

"Thanks a lot, Mom! Now I have to make a whole new one. And Joe's coming over to pick me up for the game any minute."

Emma slipped into the house. She heard the stomp of Michael's feet on the stairs. His bedroom door slammed.

Mrs. Benson was folding clean clothes on the kitchen table. "It's my fault," she said. "I never should have put that shirt in the dryer."

"Where is it now?" Emma asked.

Her mother sighed. "In the garbage pail."

Michael's door was still closed. Emma shut her bedroom door, too, before she put on the shirt. Then she straightened her baseball cap and looked at herself in the mirror on the back of her closet door.

The shirt fit perfectly. The letters had hardly faded at all. She twisted around to see the back. The bombs falling out of the plane were as black as ever.

She liked the T-shirt tucked in, but hanging out looked even better. More professional. Emma rolled up the cuffs of her jeans so her white socks showed above her sneakers. She grinned at the new Boonsville Bomber in the mirror.

Then, even though it was hot, she put on her old corduroy jacket and buttoned it up. She didn't want Michael to see the shirt right away. She wanted it to be a surprise.

But Michael didn't come down for lunch. He was still upstairs in his room when Joe came banging through the front door. He wore his Bombers T-shirt and his lucky wristbands and his lucky red socks.

"Hi, Pee-wee," he said to Emma. He rubbed the top of her baseball cap. "Where's Mike?"

Emma ducked her head. Joe was Michael's best friend and the best home-run hitter on the team, but Emma hated it when he called her Pee-wee.

"He's not feeling too well," Mrs. Benson said. Emma wasn't sure her mother liked Joe all that much, either. Once she overheard her talking about him to Mr. Benson. "That boy thinks he's the cat's pajamas," she'd said.

"But he can't be sick," Joe said. "Then we'll have to bring Weasel Malloy in to play first base and we won't have any outfielders at all."

"Hey, Joe. That you?" Michael clattered down the stairs. "I'm all set."

Joe stared at him. "What's with your T-shirt?" he asked. "It looks brand-new."

Michael pounded a fist into his glove. "I'll mess it up at the game," he said. There were Magic Marker stains on his fingers.

"Did you hear about Owen Zabriskie?" Joe

asked. "He got a single and a double yesterday. That makes 2,994 career hits."

"Yeah. But the Pioneers lost anyway. Now they're seven games out of first place. And Zabriskie is all we've got."

"I get to carry the stuff," Joe said.

"But you carried it last time."

"And I'm going to carry it this time, too," Joe said.

Michael handed him the old laundry bag with BOONSVILLE BOMBERS EQUIPMENT stenciled on it in capital letters.

Emma followed them out the door. They didn't notice her until they reached the sidewalk.

"Hey, Mike, I think your kid sister's tailing us," Joe said.

"Beat it, Emma," Michael said.

"It's okay," Emma said. "I can come with you." She peeled off her jacket.

Michael stopped dead on the sidewalk. His mouth dropped open.

"Surprise!" Emma said.

"How'd she get that shirt?" Joe said. "No one can have a shirt who's not on the team."

"I guess it's my old one," Michael said. He didn't look too happy. "I threw it away."

"And I found it," Emma said. "So now I can play."

Joe glared at Michael. "What's she talking about?"

"Nothing," Michael said. "I sort of told her, that's all."

"No girls," Joe said. "That's the rule."

"I'll play with you later, okay, Em?" Michael said.

"But I have a shirt. And you said . . ."

Michael looked at Joe. "Maybe we could put her in the field. With Weasel. Just for a couple of outs?"

"Have you ever seen a girl play?" Joe said. "They can't catch. They scream when they see a fly ball coming. And they can't throw.

They've got arms like chicken wings." Joe flapped his elbows and squawked.

Emma stared at her sneakers.

"She's not that bad," Michael said.

"And they're bad luck," Joe said. "Everybody knows that. I'm not playing on any team with some dumb girl. And it's my bat, remember? So beat it, Pee-wee!" He shouldered the equipment bag and turned away.

"I guess you'd better go home," Michael said.

Emma went slowly back up the walk to the house.

It wasn't fair. She knew she threw better than a chicken. She threw almost as well as Joe and a lot better than Weasel Malloy.

Why hadn't Michael told Joe that? He should have made Joe let her play. He'd promised. He should have stood up for her.

She kicked a stone into the flower bed. Then she sat down on the front steps with her chin in her hands. She wished the sun would stop shining. She wished a big black thundercloud would zap right over the Bombers' heads and rain their stupid ball game out.

# CHAPTER THREE

Emma sat on the steps all afternoon.

"Would you like to help me make choc-olate-chip cookies?" Mrs. Benson asked.

"No," Emma said.

"Well, why don't you get your tennis ball and bang it against the house?" Mrs. Benson suggested.

"Michael stinks," Emma muttered.

"How about some warm cookies and milk?" Mrs. Benson asked a while later.

"I'm not hungry," Emma said.

She glared at the mail truck when it stopped in front of her house. The mailman raised the red flag on the mailbox and drove away.

Emma stared at the red flag for a long time. Finally, she got up and went to see.

The mailbox was stuffed full. She pulled out a magazine and a newspaper and an important-looking letter for her father. Then she pulled out a package wrapped in brown paper.

The package was addressed to her, from Aunt Esther in New York City.

Emma stuffed everything else back into the mailbox and tore off the brown paper.

Inside was a beat-up-looking box tied with red ribbon and a letter.

*Dear Emma,* the letter read, *In New York City there are two baseball teams, the Yankees and the Mets. But I'm going to keep rooting for the Indiana Pioneers. Isn't Owen*

*Zabriskie wonderful? Love, Aunt Esther. P.S. When I opened my closet door this morning, these fell out on my head. So I am passing them on to you.*

Emma pulled off the ribbon and lifted the lid. The box was full of baseball cards!

"Well, look at that," Mrs. Benson said. "Esther always was the athletic one."

"There are hundreds of them, Mom," Emma said. "And some of them are really old." She began to lay the cards out in lines on the kitchen table. "But they're all perfect!"

"I remember that one." Mrs. Benson leaned over Emma's shoulder. "That's Ted Williams. Your aunt Esther talked about him all the time. He never tipped his hat, no matter how much the crowd cheered. I think he's retired now."

"And, Mom, here's Owen Zabriskie." Emma peered at the picture. Owen Zabriskie stood at the plate about to swing. "But he's got a mustache. He doesn't have a mustache now."

"He must have shaved it off," Mrs. Benson said.

Mr. Benson came into the kitchen carrying the rest of the mail. He stopped when he saw the kitchen table. It was covered with cards.

"Where did those come from?" he asked.

"Aunt Esther," Emma said. "She sent them to me because of her closet."

Mr. Benson whistled through his teeth. "That's some collection! Look, there's Willie Mays, the Say-Hey Kid. Why, she's even got a Pete Reiser."

"Who was he?" Emma asked.

"He was an old Brooklyn Dodger," Mr. Benson said. "He used to knock himself out against the wall trying to catch long fly balls."

"I think Esther was in love with Ted Williams," Mrs. Benson said.

"Well, I've got a surprise, too." Mr. Benson held up an envelope. "Three tickets to the Pioneers' game next Saturday."

"A real game? At the stadium?" asked Emma.

"Yup. A real game."

"I've never been to a real game before."

"It's a lot better than on TV," Mr. Benson said.

"But why only three tickets?" Emma asked.

"It's a waste of money to buy one for me," Mrs. Benson said. "I'd just fall asleep. Now, pick up your cards, Emma. I have to set the table."

That night at supper, Michael just poked at his peas and chicken. "How come Emma gets to keep all those cards," he asked, "and I don't get any? She's my aunt, too, you know."

"You've been collecting your own cards," Mr. Benson reminded him.

"But most of mine are cellos or wax packs. She even has an Owen Zabriskie."

"You've got one, too," Mr. Benson said.

"But mine's new. Hers is his *rookie* card!" Michael said. "And it's in mint condition. It must be worth a ton of money."

"I don't want to sell it," Emma said. "I want to keep them all."

"Then I want my Bombers shirt back," Michael said.

"But you threw it away."

"It's still mine," Michael said.

"Do I have to, Mom?" Emma asked.

"No more about that shirt, Michael," Mrs. Benson said. "Emma found it. It's hers now."

"Why don't you bring your Owen Zabriskie card to the stadium on Saturday?" Mr. Benson said to Michael. "Maybe we can get him to autograph it after the game."

"Hey, that's right," Michael said. "Can we go early, Dad, and stay late?"

After supper, Emma went upstairs to write Aunt Esther a thank-you letter. She was sitting at her desk in her pajamas and her baseball cap when Michael came into her room.

"How would you like to make a trade?" Michael said.

"What trade?"

Michael closed the door behind him. "If you give me one of your cards, I'll fix it so you can play in a Bombers game. Okay?"

Emma looked down at her letter. She had only gotten as far as *Dear Aunt Esther*. "Which card?" she asked.

"Only your Owen Zabriskie," Michael said.

"But that's one of my best," Emma said.

"Well, if you don't want to play, forget it," Michael said.

"I do want to play," Emma said. "More than anything."

"So, are you going to trade or what?" Michael asked. "Is it a deal?"

Emma pictured Owen Zabriskie's face on the card with his little mustache curling up at the ends. "Okay," she said finally. "It's a deal."

# CHAPTER FOUR

When Emma woke up the next day, it was raining. She worried all morning, but by early afternoon the rain had stopped. Emma pulled her baseball cap down to her eyebrows and went to wait for Michael in the front hall.

"Is Joe coming to pick us up?" she asked.

Michael shook his head.

"Then can I carry the equipment bag?" Emma asked.

"No," Michael said. "That wasn't part of the deal."

There were puddles on the sidewalk and puddles on the shortcut path that ran behind the used car lot.

"Slow down, Mikey," Emma said. "You're going too fast."

"That's the deal," Michael said. "And don't call me Mikey."

When they got to the old ball field in back of their school, Ben Winooski and Spike Johnson and Weasel Malloy were sitting in the empty wooden bleachers.

"Hey, Emma," Weasel said. "Great shirt! Are you going to cheerlead?"

"Rah, rah, sis boom bah," chanted Ben.

"No," Emma said. "I'm going to play."

"Who says?" asked Spike.

Michael was rummaging around in the equipment bag.

"Tell them, Michael," Emma said.

Everyone looked at Michael. Spike

stopped smiling. "Does Joe know?" he asked.

"He won't like it," Ben said.

"I can handle him," Michael said.

"Well, it's okay by me," said Weasel. "We could use some help. Like in the outfield."

Michael laid out the metal bat, an old catcher's mask, three gloves, and a water bottle. "We might as well start," he said.

"Great," Weasel said. "If Joe's not coming, I get to use a glove."

"I'll pitch," Michael said. "You want to be up first, Spike?"

Spike looked at Emma. "I guess so," he said.

"She can play left field," Michael said. "Okay, you guys?"

"Okay," said Weasel.

"Watch it," Ben said. "Here comes Joe."

"Go on out to the field," Michael told Emma.

Emma trotted across the scruffy wet grass.

When she figured she was out far enough, she turned around.

All the Bombers were crowded around home plate. Joe's fists were on his hips and he was yelling. She saw him kick the dirt. Then she saw Michael talking to him alone by the bleachers. Finally, Ben put on the catcher's mask and Spike went out to the mound. Michael ran down the line to first base.

Joe stood at the plate slashing the air with his bat.

Weasel jogged toward her. He wasn't wearing a glove. "Boy, is he mad," he said. "You'd better move way back. He'll probably hit it a mile."

"How long does he get to bat?" Emma asked.

"Until he flies out or gets tagged out running," Weasel said. "Or strikes out. But he never does that. He'll probably be up all afternoon. And I'm batting fourth."

Spike's first pitch was high and outside. His second pitch was right over the plate. "Strike one!" bellowed Ben.

Emma stared in from the field. Spike went into his windup again.

Joe gave a mighty swing.

Emma heard the clack of the metal bat hitting the ball. She saw the ball come sailing out toward her. It was hit high, but not that far. Emma started to run. The white speck in the sky was the size of a snowflake. Then it was the size of a snowball. The ball was coming down too fast. It was going to drop in for a hit.

At the very last moment Emma dove.

Water sprayed up all around her. And then she felt something hard and round plunk into her outstretched hands.

"She caught it!" Weasel yelled. "I don't believe it! Shoestring catch."

Emma climbed to her feet. Her hands still stung and her Bombers T-shirt was sopping,

but she didn't care. She held up the ball so Michael could see.

Joe rounded first base. He headed for home.

"Stop running," Spike shouted. "You're out."

"Throw it here," Ben bellowed.

"You're out! You're out!" Weasel shrieked.

Joe rounded first base again.

Emma reared back and threw as hard as she could. The ball shot past Spike and hit the dirt right in front of the plate. It bounced into Ben's glove just as Joe barreled into him. They both went down in a heap.

Emma saw the ball pop out of Ben's glove and dribble toward the backstop.

"Safe!" Joe shouted. "I'm safe. Inside-the-park home run!"

"No way!" Weasel came tearing in from the field. "She caught it. I saw her. You're totally out."

Joe straddled the plate. "She did not. It hit the ground first. She trapped it."

"She caught it, Joe," Spike said. "I saw her, too."

"You couldn't see an elephant if it sat on your nose," Joe shouted.

Emma wished Joe would stop yelling and just be out.

"Tell him," she said to Michael. "It landed right in my hands."

"Come on, Joe," Michael said. "Give Ben the bat. He's up next."

"Okay, he can be up," Joe said. "If you sissies want to believe a girl, it's okay by me. But I'm not sticking around." He shouldered the bat and marched off.

For a while, everyone just stood around home plate. No one said anything. Finally Ben picked up the catcher's mask. "I guess that's the ball game," he said.

Spike dumped the water bottle and the

catcher's mask back into the equipment bag. No one looked at Emma.

"You mean we aren't going to play anymore?" Emma asked.

"He's got the only bat," Michael said.

"But I only got to catch once and throw once," Emma said. "And you said if I traded I could play a whole game."

"That was the whole game," Michael said.

# CHAPTER FIVE

The next day Emma sat at her desk finishing her letter to Aunt Esther.

*It wasn't a whole game at all,* she wrote. *It was only the littlest bit of a game. But Joe won't let me play anymore. He says he'll take his bat away forever next time. And Michael never stands up for me. Not ever. He won't even give my Owen Zabriskie card back. He says a trade's a trade. So please write him and tell him he has to. And tell him he has to make Joe stop calling me Pee-wee. Love, Emma. P.S. I am going to a real baseball game this Saturday. Owen Zabriskie will be in it. Michael says he is going to try to get him to sign my card. So please write back right away.*

She folded the pages and went to ask for an envelope and a lot of stamps. "It has to get there really fast," she explained.

"Then we'd better send it Express Mail," Mrs. Benson said.

"Where's my Bombers T-shirt?" Emma asked, when they got back from the post office.

"In the dryer," Mrs. Benson said. "But I couldn't get rid of the grass stain."

"I like the grass stain," Emma said.

Michael was at his Bombers game. Emma fished her old tennis ball out of the umbrella stand and went to practice in the backyard. But practicing by herself wasn't that much fun anymore. She kept remembering Joe's fly ball and how white it had looked dropping out of the clear blue sky. She remembered Weasel yelling, "I don't believe it!" and Ben waving his arms at her from home plate.

Mrs. Benson came out on the back porch. She wiped her hands on her apron. "Throw me that ball," she said. "Your Aunt Esther used to play catch with me when we were little."

"That's okay," Emma said. "You don't have to."

"Throw it. Esther used to say I was pretty good."

"She did? You were?"

"Try me," Mrs. Benson said.

Emma threw a nice soft lob. Mrs. Benson gave a little shriek and stuck out her arms. The ball bounced off her fingers. Mrs. Benson chased it across the yard. "Oh, dear," she said. "I guess I'm a bit rusty. Get ready now. I'm going to hurl it back to you."

"I'm ready," Emma said.

Mrs. Benson wiped the ball on her apron. She planted her feet. She wound up and threw. The ball bounced three times and rolled between Emma's legs.

Emma stared at her mother.

"You missed it," Mrs. Benson said.

Emma just stood there. Why had Aunt Esther said her mother was good? Her mother was terrible. She threw exactly like a chicken.

"Well, aren't you going to go get it?" Mrs. Benson said. "Come on. Let's have a little get-up-and-go, here."

Emma turned slowly around and picked up the ball. Maybe *she* really threw like that, too. Maybe girls couldn't play. Her shoe-string catch could have been just luck. When Michael said she was good, maybe he meant for a girl.

Maybe Joe was right.

Mrs. Benson was waiting with her arms stuck out exactly like the first time.

"I'm tired," Emma said. "I don't feel like playing anymore."

That night, Emma saw Owen Zabriskie get his 2,996th hit on television. The next night, he hit numbers 2,997 and 2,998. Number 2,998 was a home run. Mr. Benson cheered and pounded the arm of the flowered sofa. "Only two more to go!" he kept saying. "Maybe he'll get his 3,000th tomorrow. When we're at the game."

"Yeah, maybe," Michael mumbled.

Emma wasn't cheering, either. She was wondering whether girls batted like chickens, too.

"What's wrong with you guys?" Mr. Benson asked. "Why are you both so quiet?"

Michael didn't answer.

Emma pulled the brim of her baseball cap down over her eyes.

"Emma," Mrs. Benson called from the hall. "The telephone's for you."

Emma climbed slowly off the sofa. Mrs.

Benson held out the receiver. "Hello," Emma said.

"Hi, Emma."

"Hello, Aunt Esther." Aunt Esther's voice sounded as if she was calling from the house next door. "Are you still in New York City?"

"I'm still here. And I got your letter."

"That's okay," Emma said. "I don't think it matters anymore."

"Yes, it does. That's why I'm calling. Did you know that a girl is playing first base for one of the best Little League teams in the whole country?"

Emma pressed the phone against her ear. "Are you sure?"

"I'm sure. I have the article right here."

"But Joe says girls can't play. Joe says they're bad luck. And Mom . . ."

"Her name is Victoria," Aunt Esther interrupted, "and she's a terrific player."

"She is?"

"Yes, she is. So far she's only made one error and she's hit seven home runs. So phooey on Joe."

"I'll get Michael," Emma shouted. "You can tell him and then he can tell Joe."

"You tell Joe," Aunt Esther said. "You can stand up for yourself."

"But what about my Owen Zabriskie card?"

"Well, if you're asking my opinion, I think Michael is right. A trade is a trade. If a team trades for a player and that player gets hurt, even if it's in the very first game, the team can't give him back. But if you happen to see Owen Zabriskie tomorrow, shake his hand for me."

"Okay, but Aunt Esther . . ."

"What?"

Emma cupped her hand over the phone. "I was just wondering. About Mom. Did you really tell her she was a good player?"

"Yes, I did," Aunt Esther said. "It was a terrible lie. She was the worst player I ever saw in my whole life."

"She catches and throws just like a chicken," Emma whispered.

"I know. But I don't play like that. And neither does Victoria in Little League. And neither do you. Right?"

"Right," Emma said. "But what am I going to do about the Bombers?"

"I don't know," Aunt Esther said. "You're going to have to figure that one out for yourself."

# CHAPTER
# SIX

The sun poured in through the windows on Saturday morning. Emma sat at the kitchen table in her pajamas and her baseball cap trying to drown her Cheerios in milk.

Michael wasn't eating. "What time is it?" he asked.

"Nine o'clock. I just told you," said Mrs. Benson.

"We'd better get going, Dad," Michael said.

Mr. Benson lowered his newspaper. "It's only an hour's drive to the stadium and the game doesn't start until two."

"But I want to be there before anyone. Owen Zabriskie likes to take early batting practice. He's probably there already."

"Owen Zabriskie is probably still asleep," Mr. Benson said.

"But, Dad, we could have a flat tire or get caught in a traffic jam. . . ."

"Calm down, Michael. What's gotten into you this morning? Are you trying to drive your mother and me crazy?"

"I'm not going to wear a dress to the game," Emma said.

Michael bombed his Cheerios with a slice of banana.

"If we don't leave soon," he said, "we probably won't have time to fill out our scorecards or anything."

"You've got hours yet," Mrs. Benson told him. "What are you worrying about?"

Michael dropped another banana bomb. "Nothing," he mumbled.

Upstairs, Emma made her bed and pulled on her jeans. She rolled up the cuffs so her white socks showed. Then she put on her grass-stained Boonsville Bombers T-shirt and began to sort through her box of baseball cards.

From the backyard came the drone of a lawn mower. After a while, the sound moved around to the front of the house. The screen door banged and she heard Michael's voice. "Dad, it's *really* late. So can we go now? Please."

The mower slowed to a *putt-putt*. "Not until I've finished this lawn."

"I'm going to wait in the car," Michael said.

Emma put away her cards and went downstairs. Her father circled the front lawn behind the mower. "Almost done," he called, and waved to her.

Michael was hunched down in the back-seat of the station wagon. Emma could see the top of his black baseball cap. She peered in through the half-open window.

"What time is it now?" Michael asked.

"It's not even twelve o'clock yet," Emma said. "I checked in the kitchen."

"That's too late." Michael slid lower in the seat. "We'll never get out of here before he comes."

"Who?"

"Joe. And it's all your fault."

"Why? What did I do?"

"You made me let you play with the Bombers, that's what," Michael said.

"I did not make you. We traded for it."

"Yeah, but Joe wasn't going to let you play no matter what, so I had to promise. Or I would have had to give you your Owen Za-briskie card back."

"Promise what?"

Michael stared at his knees. "That he

could go to the Pioneers' game with me."

"You mean the Pioneers' game today?"

Michael nodded. "And if he doesn't get to come, he'll probably fix it so I can't play with the Bombers, either."

"But how could you? Dad only got three tickets."

"I know that." Suddenly Michael straight-ened up and stuck his head out the window. "So listen, Emma. You could let Joe have your ticket. Okay? I'll make your bed for two whole weeks if you do."

Emma shook her head.

"And I'll play catch with you, twice a day for the rest of the summer. And you can use one of the gloves from the equipment bag, if you don't tell Joe."

"But it's my ticket," Emma said. "And I've never been to a game before." The lawn mower racketed past the flower bed behind her.

"You can have mine next time," Michael said. "And if you want, I'll even teach you how to bat."

"No," Emma said.

The lawn mower cut off. "I'll be with you in a minute, kids," Mr. Benson hollered.

"Come on, Emma. Please! Joe will be here any minute."

"He's here now," Emma said.

Joe turned in at the driveway. He was wearing his lucky wristbands and his lucky socks.

"Oh, brother," Michael said. He rolled up the window and ducked out of sight. Emma opened the front door of the station wagon and climbed in. "Don't tell him where I am," Michael whispered from the backseat.

"Hi, Mr. Benson," Joe said. "Great day for the game."

"Oh, hello, Joe," Mr. Benson said. "Michael's in the car."

Emma pretended the car was moving. She pretended they were driving into the parking lot at the game. She pictured the way the stadium looked on television, with flags waving all around the top and the big scoreboard that lit up after a home run.

Joe's sneakers crunched on the gravel and then she heard him knock on Michael's window.

"Hey, Mike. Open up. It's me."

"Oh, Joe," Michael said. "I guess I fell asleep."

"Unlock the door," Joe ordered.

"I can't. I think it's stuck."

Joe's sneakers crunched around behind the car and then Emma heard the other door open. "What's Pee-wee doing here?" Joe asked. "I thought she wasn't coming."

"She wasn't," Michael said. "But now she is."

"I can handle that," Joe said. "Zabriskie

probably won't get his 3,000th, though. Not with her along."

"Then there's no point in your coming," Michael said.

"What do you mean by that?"

"Well, here's the thing. I just found out there aren't enough tickets."

"For who?"

"For you," Michael said.

"Forget that. We made a deal and I've got it all planned." Joe climbed into the backseat and slammed the door. "Besides, there's nobody home at my house. They've all gone to visit my grandmother. So I'm coming, like it or not."

"You can't. You've got to get out."

"Make me," Joe said.

"Okay, kids," Mr. Benson settled himself behind the wheel. "Game time. Everybody ready to go?"

"I'm ready," Emma said.

"Can we drop you anywhere, Joe?"

"No," Joe said. "I'm coming with you. Mike invited me."

Mr. Benson turned around and stared at Michael. "You want to tell me what's going on here?" he said.

Emma imagined herself in the stands as Owen Zabriskie came to the plate, swishing his bat. The bases were loaded. The pitcher shook off a sign. The crowd grew quiet. Owen Zabriskie dug his back foot into the dirt of the batter's box and waited, absolutely still.

"Well, I was really looking forward to this game," Mr. Benson said. "So I guess there's only one thing to do."

"I'm going," Emma said.

"So am I," said Joe.

"We're all going," Mr. Benson said. "I'll just have to buy an extra ticket when we get there."

Michael let out a big breath. "Gee, Dad. Great! Thanks!"

"You're welcome," Mr. Benson said. "Now everyone buckle up."

"Have a good time," Mrs. Benson called from the front steps.

Emma leaned out her window. "I will!" she shouted.

# CHAPTER
# SEVEN

At the stadium, Emma waited with Michael and Joe while Mr. Benson stood in line at the ticket window. All around her people streamed toward the entrance gates. "One size fits all! Get 'em while they're hot!" yelled a man selling Pioneers' caps.

Mr. Benson threaded his way through the crowd. He was shaking his head.

"Sold out," he said.

Michael groaned. "Not even standing room?"

"They're hanging from the rafters in there," Mr. Benson said. "Because of Owen Zabriskie."

"Just our luck," Joe muttered. He glared at Emma.

"So here are the tickets," Mr. Benson said to Michael. "Don't lose them." Then he pulled out his wallet. "And fifteen dollars for hot dogs and soda."

Michael stared at the three tickets in his hand. "I guess you ought to take mine, Dad," he said.

"That's okay," Mr. Benson put a hand on Michael's shoulder. "I'm going to go back to the car and listen to the game on the radio. It's almost as good that way. But remember, I'll meet you right outside Gate 13 when it's over. And you two boys take care of Emma."

"I promise," Michael said.

"Get along with you now or you'll be late."

Emma watched her father start back toward the parking lot. Everyone else was headed in the other direction.

"Come on." Michael tugged at her arm.

"I want a program," Joe said as soon as they were through the turnstile. Michael asked for three little yellow pencils. "We're going to share," he explained to the program man. "There's a scorecard in the back," he told Emma. "We can take turns."

"I get to carry it," Joe said.

Emma was swept along by the crowd, past refreshment stands with their spicy smell of hot dogs and mustard and up one ramp after another. Finally Michael said, "That's us, Section 24."

Emma followed him through a short tunnel. Then she stopped and stood blinking in the sunlight.

It was as if the tunnel were a magic hole and she had popped out of it into a dream.

She saw a bowl of blue sky over her head, much bluer than on television, and bright flags, much brighter than on television, rippling in the wind. She saw the curve of the stands filled with people. But mostly she saw the grass of the ball field.

Never in her life had she seen anything so thick, so even, so green.

"Move it, Pee-wee," Joe said. "We'll be late for the National Anthem."

"Hurry up, Emma," Michael said.

The usher dusted off three seats. "She can go in first," Joe said. "I want to sit on the aisle."

"Is the grass real?" Emma whispered to Michael.

"They grow it special," Michael said. "And they water it all the time."

The fat man on the other side of Emma started to whistle and cheer before "The Star-Spangled Banner" was through. But Emma hardly noticed. She stared at the ball field. The pure white bases and the white foul lines made the grass seem even greener.

Then there was a roar from the fans as the Pioneers, in their white home uniforms, charged out of the dugout.

"Hey, great seats," Joe shouted. "There's Zabriskie!"

Emma looked down. Owen Zabriskie stood below her in right field, stretching out his legs and loosening up his arm. His uniform was so white he seemed to glow in the sun.

"And the wind's blowing out," Joe said. "That means a lot of home runs probably."

"Right," Michael said.

Emma didn't say anything. All she wanted was to sit where she was forever.

There were no home runs in the first inning. But in the second inning, when Owen Zabriskie came to the plate, the crowd went wild. *"Ooooooh, Oh-wen!"* they chanted.

*"Gooooo, Oh-wen!"* The electronic scoreboard flashed his picture and the number 2,998 over and over again.

But Owen struck out. "Dumb swing," Joe said. "That pitch was in the dirt."

There were no home runs in the third inning, either, or in the fourth or fifth. Emma didn't care. She saw Owen Zabriskie make a great running catch at the warning track. She saw the shortstop snare a ball lined up the middle, flip it to the second baseman who rifled it to first for a double play. She saw the catcher fall into the stands to catch a pop foul.

"I'm hungry," Joe said at the beginning of the sixth inning. "I need another hot dog."

"You want one now?" Michael asked Emma. Emma shook her head. All she wanted was for the game never to be over.

Emma passed the fat man a soda and a pretzel and a box of Cracker Jacks and three hot dogs. He asked for extra mustards.

"It's my turn to score," Michael said to Joe.

"No way. Not until we get a run."

"But Emma needs a turn, too."

"No, I don't," Emma said. She didn't want to take her eyes off the field.

Owen Zabriskie led off for the Pioneers in the bottom half of the sixth. *"Oh, Oh-wen! Go, Oh-wen!"* the crowd chanted, and the scoreboard flashed again.

The count went to one ball and two strikes and then Owen smashed a line drive over the glove of the leaping third baseman. The left fielder chased it down in the corner. Owen rounded first and headed for second. The throw came in, but Owen was already standing on the bag.

Michael and Joe yelled and pummeled each other and jumped up and down. "Way to go, Big *Oh!*" Michael hollered. A picture of rockets exploded on the scoreboard screen and then the words *It's a Hit!* and the number 2,999*!*

Michael turned and gave Emma a high five. "Did you see that?" he shouted. "Boy, can he still fly!"

"He ran right out from under his cap," Emma said.

"He could run circles around me," the fat man said. He was bright red in the face from cheering.

Finally, the crowd quieted down and the next batter stepped into the box. Owen sidled a few steps off second base.

"Home run!" Joe yelled. "Hit it out of here!"

Emma heard the crack of the bat and saw the ball drop into center field. She watched Owen round third base. She saw the ball being relayed in. Owen slid in a cloud of dust. Safe at home!

Joe scribbled madly with his yellow pencil. By the time the inning was over the Pioneers led, 3–0.

"What did I tell you?" he crowed. "The wind's blowing out!"

"My turn to score now," Michael said.

"Okay, but just for an inning," Joe said.

The fat man bought another box of Cracker Jacks. "I always eat when we're ahead," he said to Emma.

But in the seventh inning the Pioneers' pitcher couldn't get the ball over the plate and when he did the batters clobbered it. The crowd grew silent. Run after run scored. When the inning was finally over, the Pioneers were losing, 5–3.

"They're killing us," Joe muttered.

"It's only two runs," Michael said. "There's still time."

"We never should have come with a girl," Joe fumed. "I told you they were bad luck."

"Owen could still hit one out of here," Michael said.

"Fat chance," Joe grumbled. "He'll probably strike out again. And look at the flags. Now the wind's blowing in."

Emma didn't care about the wind. And she didn't even care that much whether the Pioneers won or not. She wanted the score to be tied so the game would have to go into extra innings.

In the Pioneers' half of the eighth inning, Owen Zabriskie came up again. There were runners on first and second and two men out. A great long-drawn-out *"Oh"* filled the stadium. The fans held up an enormous hand-lettered sign in the left-field bleachers. 3 OH OH OH OH-WEN! it read.

Emma leaned forward in her seat. Late afternoon shadows covered home plate, but the grass of the outfield was still green in the sun.

The pitcher reared back and threw. Owen swung.

Emma heard the sharp crack of the bat

and a huge roar from the crowd. And then the ball came sailing straight toward her just the way it had when she was playing the outfield for the Bombers.

All around her people were leaping to their feet and reaching up. Then Emma saw the ball begin to curve to the left. There was no way she could make another shoestring catch. She reached out anyway, but the ball hit the steps behind Joe, bounced once, and rolled out of sight.

Emma scrambled after it.

The fat man was trying to squeeze down onto his knees, too. Emma felt someone step on her leg. A hand grabbed at her arm. And then she saw it, under the seat in front of her. It was lying right next to an empty Cracker Jacks box, like a big white prize.

# CHAPTER
# EIGHT

When Emma crawled out from underneath the seat, the stadium was in an uproar. Real fireworks exploded above the scoreboard and all the Pioneer players waited to mob Owen Zabriskie at home plate. The crowd was on its feet, shouting and clapping and whistling, except the fans around Emma. They were still searching for the ball.

"Mikey," Emma said.

"I almost had it!" Joe shrieked at Michael.

"Did you see? It bounced right over my head!"

"Michael," Emma said, louder.

"But where did it go?" Michael asked. "Who got it?"

"I did," Emma said.

"Well, I'll be darned." The fat man hoisted himself back into his seat.

"You did?" Michael said. "You sure?"

Emma uncurled her fingers. The ball lay in the cup of her hands.

"Emma has it, Joe! Look!"

"Did you hear that, folks," the fat man bellowed. "This lucky little lady caught the ball!"

A sea of faces turned toward Emma.

"Let me see it," Joe said.

Emma held it out. There was a dark spot, like a bruise, on the white leather.

"Gosh," Michael said. "That must be where he hit it."

"I want to hold it," Joe said. "Just for a minute."

"No," Emma said.

"Hey, we're on television!" The fat man waved his arms at the scoreboard. Emma looked up. She saw a picture of the crowd on the giant screen and then the picture zoomed in closer and she saw herself in her red baseball cap and her Bombers T-shirt. Michael and Joe and the fat man were in the picture, too, right next to her.

The picture faded and there was a new picture of Owen Zabriskie in the dugout giving everyone high fives.

"I don't believe it," Michael said. "Did you really catch it, Emma?"

Emma shook her head. People were still staring at her.

"I deflected it," Joe said. "I felt it touch my fingers."

"Heads up," said the fat man. "Here come the security guards."

Two men in brown pants and white shirts charged up the concrete steps. They both wore police-type badges and one of them carried a walkie-talkie.

"Which one of you kids caught the ball?" asked the guard with the walkie-talkie.

"I touched it," Joe said.

Another roar filled the stadium. Owen Zabriskie had come out of the dugout to tip his hat to the crowd.

"My sister did," Michael said.

"Good for you, missy. But we'll have to take it back now. We'll trade you this brand-new one instead."

Emma closed her fingers around the ball and hugged it against her stomach.

"Come on, kid. It's a real important ball. Zabriskie needs it for his trophy room."

"No," Emma said. "It's mine."

"Give it back," Joe whispered. "You want to get us in trouble?"

"But I found it," Emma said.

"Okay, missy." The guard reached into his other pocket. "We'll give you two balls for it. Two for one. That's some deal, right?"

"No," Emma said in a low voice.

"What do you say, kid?" asked the guard.

"She said no," Michael told him.

"You want to get us sent to prison?" Joe hissed.

"You her father?" the guard asked the fat man.

"My father's in the parking lot," Michael said. "He's going to be waiting for us at Gate 13."

The people around them began to murmur and shift in their seats.

The guard unhooked his walkie-talkie. Emma heard the crackle of static. "We found the kid," the guard said into the mouthpiece. "But she won't give it up. Ask the boss what he wants us to do."

Emma pulled the brim of her baseball cap

over her eyes. She tried not to listen to the squawks coming out of the black box.

"Yes, sir. Right away, sir," the guard said into the walkie-talkie. Then he turned to Emma. "Okay, miss. Let's go."

"But the game's not over," Emma clutched the ball tighter. She wished her father was there instead of Joe or the fat man.

"It's over for you," the guard said.

"I'm going with her," Michael said.

"Where are you taking us?" Joe asked.

"Why don't you leave the little girl alone," said the fat man.

"This way," the guard said to Emma. Michael crowded into the aisle next to her. The other guard closed in behind Joe. They all went down the concrete steps.

"Way to go, kid!" someone yelled at Emma.

"Hang in there," yelled someone else.

"Keep moving," ordered the guard.

At the entrance to the tunnel, Emma heard another roar from the crowd. She looked back. The teams were changing sides. She caught a last glimpse of the Pioneers running out onto the bright green field.

# CHAPTER NINE

"I told you she'd get us in trouble," Joe said. "Now what are we going to do?"

Emma looked around the small, cluttered office. Papers covered the big desk and all the pictures on the wall hung crooked. She guessed that they were somewhere in the basement of the stadium.

"Dad will come and find us," Michael said.

"Why didn't you just give them their dumb ball?" Joe glowered at Emma.

"It isn't theirs anymore," Emma said. "It was in the stands." She rubbed her fingers along the seams of the baseball and stared at the pictures. Most of them were of past Pioneers' teams with the dates of the years printed underneath.

"Maybe we could make a run for it," Michael said.

"How stupid can you get," Joe said. "The guards are right outside."

Emma could see them through the window in the door.

"Well, anyway, the game's got to be over soon," Michael said. "Then they'll have to let us go."

"I'm not spending the night here, that's for sure," Joe said.

"Stuff it," Michael said. "Someone's coming."

Emma heard a murmur of voices and the clatter of baseball cleats on the floor. There was a burst of laughter and shouting right outside the door. "Okay, you guys, later," a voice said. "I've got to take care of this first."

Michael moved closer to Emma.

Then the door opened. Owen Zabriskie came into the room.

"Oh, brother," Michael gasped. "It's him!"

He looked gigantic to Emma. From the stands he had seemed normal-sized because the field was so huge, but now he looked even bigger than on television. His cap was pushed back on his head and there was a towel draped around his neck.

"Keep everyone out of here for a few minutes, will you?" Owen Zabriskie said to the guards and closed the door.

Emma stared up at him. She could hear Michael breathing. Owen Zabriskie studied them for a moment. "So who am I dealing with here?" he asked finally.

"I guess me," Emma said. Her voice sounded funny.

"I've got to sit down," Owen Zabriskie said. "My knees aren't as good as they used to be."

"Here," Joe said. "Use my chair."

Owen Zabriskie sat down with a sigh. One leg of his white pants was stained with dirt from his slide into home plate.

"That was a great home run, Mr. Zabriskie," Michael said. "The greatest."

"I got lucky," Owen said. "He threw me a hanging fastball right on the outside corner." He wiped his face with the towel and looked at Emma. "You must have made some catch."

"I didn't catch it," Emma said. "I fielded it."

"Oh, so you're a ball player, too," Owen said. He stared at her T-shirt. "A Boonsville Bomber? I used to play Little League. Is that the name of your team?"

"It's not Little League," Emma said. "It's my brother Michael and Joe and Spike and

Ben and Weasel. I play the outfield sometimes with Weasel."

"Weasel?" Owen Zabriskie grinned at her.
When he smiled he looked like the picture
on his rookie card, except for the missing
mustache. "Weasel?" he repeated, and then
he began to laugh. "Tell me about you and
Weasel."

So Emma told him about the Boonsville
Bombers. "There are only four gloves, so
Weasel doesn't get one," she explained.

"That's rough," Owen said.

"I don't have one, either, but I made a
shoestring catch," Emma told him. "And Joe
has the only bat."

"Who's Joe?"

"That's Joe," Emma pointed. "And that's
my brother, Michael. He's a really good first
baseman."

"Nice to meet you," Owen said. He turned
back to Emma. "So you all take turns with
the bat?"

"Sort of," Emma said.

Someone knocked on the door. Owen sighed. "That's the press. Tell them to hold their horses," he said to Michael. "Tell them I'm busy."

"Yes, sir." Michael went to the door and opened it a crack. "Mr. Zabriskie says he's busy. He wants you to hold your horses," he shouted and slammed the door again.

"I guess we'd better get down to business," Owen said to Emma. "What's your name, anyway? I don't think we've been properly introduced."

"Emma Lee Benson."

"Well, Emma Lee Benson, could I have a look at that ball you fielded?"

Emma went and stood beside his chair. "You can see the mark where you hit it," she said.

Owen nodded. Up close he looked a little tired. "I've still got the ball from my first major-league hit," he said, "and this is just about as important to me as that one. So, Emma Lee, do you think you and I could make a trade?"

"Okay," Emma said.

"I'll give you a whole box of new balls for it," Owen said.

Emma didn't answer. She was wondering how many balls were in a box.

"And an extra bat for the Boonsville Bombers," Owen said. "And a glove for you."

Emma didn't know what to say. A glove! A real major-league glove was better than any glove she'd ever seen at the mall.

"You drive a hard bargain," Owen said. "What if I add a glove for Weasel? I don't want to forget Weasel."

"For Weasel, too?" Emma said.

Owen looked up at Joe. "Go tell them I need a dozen balls and a bat and a couple of gloves. And tell them to make those gloves size small."

Joe went to the door. Michael nudged Emma's shoulder. "My card," he whispered.

"Oh," Emma said. "There's something else."

Owen smiled. "I figured I wasn't out of the woods yet."

"It's my brother. He has your rookie card and he wants you to sign it."

"That's an easy one," Owen said. "Get me a pen off the desk."

"Gee, thanks, Mr. Zabriskie," Michael said.

Joe came back. He was loaded with equipment.

"Anything else?" asked Owen.

"Well," Emma said. "There's my aunt Esther. She lives in New York City, but she still roots for the Pioneers. She said to say hello."

"You say hello back from me," Owen said. "And you can give her this." He pulled off his cap. "That's all I've got, except for my shoes. So, Emma Lee, do we have a deal?"

Someone pounded on the door. Mr. Benson's worried face peered through the glass.

"Yes," Emma said. "It's a deal." And she dropped Owen Zabriskie's 3,000th-hit ball into his outstretched hand.

# CHAPTER
# TEN

*So*, *I'm a real Boonsville Bomber now,* Emma wrote at the end of her letter to her Aunt Esther. *They voted me in. Joe didn't raise his hand but Weasel said he would have voted for me no matter what. Even if I hadn't given him the glove. So far I have played four times. I haven't made an error yet, but my hitting is really bad. I strike out every time.*

"Emma," Michael bellowed from downstairs. "Joe's here."

"I'm coming," Emma shouted back. *I have to go and play baseball now*, she wrote, *but I hope you like the cap. If it doesn't fit in your closet, you could hang it on your wall, maybe. Or wear it to work even. I'd wear it if it was my hat, but I've already got one. Love, Emma.*

"Hurry up," Michael yelled. "We're going to be late."

Emma had wrapped Owen Zabriskie's cap in tissue paper and tied it with a pink ribbon. She stuck the letter under the bow. Then she jammed her cap down to her eyebrows and picked up her Owen Zabriskie glove. It was as big as a shovel.

Michael and Joe were waiting by the front door.

"I get to carry the equipment bag," Joe said.

"No," Michael said. "Emma carried it yesterday, so it's my turn today."

"Then I get to carry it tomorrow," Joe said.

Michael lifted the bag. "It's a lot heavier than it used to be."

When they got to the ball field, Spike and Ben and Weasel were doing stretching exercises on the dusty grass in front of the bleachers.

"Hey, Emma," Ben called. "Owen Zabriskie got a couple more hits last night. Did you watch the game?"

"Most of it," Emma said.

"When you're hot, you're hot," Spike said.

Emma nodded. She wished she could get hot. Or even a little bit warm. She wondered if Owen Zabriskie had ever struck out eight times in a row.

"Who bats first?" Weasel asked.

"Spike does," Michael told him.

"Then me," Joe said.

"Then Emma," Michael said. "And then Weasel and then Ben and then me."

"That's okay," Emma said. "I'll go last."

"You're just in a slump," Weasel said, as they trotted toward the outfield. His Owen Zabriskie glove looked as long as his arm. "I was in a slump once."

"You were?"

"Sure. Not as bad as yours, though. But don't worry. You'll break out of it someday."

"I wish I knew what I was doing wrong," Emma said.

Spike got a single. Joe got two singles and a home run. Weasel flied out to Emma. Ben popped out to Spike. Michael hit a double before he fouled out to Joe.

"You're up," Weasel said.

Emma jogged in from the field.

She rubbed some dirt on her hands. She straightened her cap. Then she picked up the bat Owen Zabriskie had traded her and stepped into the batter's box.

Joe crouched behind the plate.

"Everybody hits!" Michael yelled from first base.

Spike wound up and pitched. Emma swung and missed.

"Strike one!" Joe yelled.

Emma stepped away from the plate. She wondered if anyone in history had ever struck out nine times in a row.

Joe threw the ball back. "You're never going to get a hit," he said. "Swinging like that."

"Like what?" As soon as she said it, Emma was sorry she'd asked. She knew he was going to say, "Like a chicken."

Joe went into his crouch again. "You're swinging too early," he muttered.

"What?"

"You're way out in front of the ball." Joe's voice was so low Emma could hardly hear him. "Wait till it gets to you. But don't say I told you."

"Okay," Emma said.

Joe stared out at Spike and pounded the pocket of his catcher's mitt. "Let me see some heat," he yelled.

Spike pitched. Emma swung. The ball bounced foul. Michael fielded it.

"I told you, wait," Joe muttered from behind his catcher's mask. "Watch the ball and wait."

Emma nodded.

Spike went into his windup. Emma watched the ball from the moment it left his hand and waited. At the very last second, she swung.

She heard a sharp *thwack* and felt a shiver in her fingers. The ball sailed over the pitcher's head. Emma dropped the bat. Weasel started back toward the faraway fence. But even before she knew for sure that Weasel was never going to make the catch, Emma was off and running.